Wait and See

story by
Robert Munsch

art by
Michael Martchenko

annick press
toronto • new york • vancouver

On the day of Olivia's birthday, her mother made a big cake and said, "Make a wish and blow them out."

Olivia really liked snow, and even though it was a warm summer day, she decided to wish for snow. She wanted it to be really deep, so she wished for **SNOW, SNOW, and more SNOW**.

Then she took a deep breath:
Ahhhhhhhhh,

and blew out the candles:
Whhhhhhhhhhhhw.

Her father said, "Well, Olivia, what did you wish for?"

Olivia said, "I wished for **SNOW, SNOW, and more SNOW**."

"Now, look next door," said her father, "you can't wish for snow. It's summertime! It doesn't snow in summertime. This is not going to work."

Olivia said, "Wait and see."

When the party was over and the kids were ready to go home, they opened the front door. There was snow at the bottom of the door, snow at the middle of the door, and snow at the top of the door. The whole house was covered with snow.

Olivia ran into the kitchen and yelled, "Mommy– Daddy, Mommy– Daddy, Mommy– Daddy; **SNOW, SNOW and more SNOW**."

The mother and father said, "Snow in the summertime? This kid is going totally nuts!" Then they opened the front door and yelled, **"AHHHHHHHHHHHH!"**

"Olivia, you have to get rid of this. This is entirely too much snow."

"Make me another birthday cake," said Olivia.

So they made Olivia another birthday cake and Olivia made a wish.

Then she took a deep breath:
Ahhhhhhhhh,

and blew out the candles:
Whhhhhhhhhhhhw.

Right away it started to rain. It rained and it rained and it washed all the snow away. "Good wish," said her father. "You wished for rain."

It rained some more and the front yard filled up with water.

"How much rain did she wish for?" asked her mother.

"Olivia," said her father, "did you wish **one** word?"

"No," said Olivia.

"Olivia," said her father, "did you wish **two** words?"

"No," said Olivia.

"Olivia," said her father, "did you wish **three** words?"

"Yes," said Olivia, "I wished for **RAIN, RAIN, and more RAIN**."

"OH, NO!" yelled her mother. Both Olivia's parents ran into the kitchen and made another birthday cake and put candles on the top. Then her mother said, "Now, Olivia, this time just wish for **one** word: SUNSHINE. That's all. Just **SUNSHINE**." So that's what Olivia did. She wished for **SUNSHINE**.

Then she took a deep breath:
Ahhhhhhhhh,

and blew out the candles:
Whhhhhhhhhhhhw.

Right away the sun came out. It got warm and all the water dried up. The mother and father went to the front yard and looked around. "This is more like it," said her mother. "Olivia wished for sunshine, just sunshine, just **one** word."

Meanwhile, back in the house, Olivia had made another birthday cake.

Then she took a deep breath:
Ahhhhhhhhh,

and blew out the candles:
Whhhhhhhhhhhhhw.

The mother and father ran in and yelled, "Olivia! Did you wish **one** word?"

"NNNNO."

"Did you wish **two** words?"

"NNNNO."

"Did you wish **three** words?"

"YYYYES."

"Oh, Olivia, what did you wish for?"

"Well," said Olivia, "I wished for **MONEY, MONEY, and more MONEY**."

"Now look," said her father, "Money is very hard stuff to get. You can't wish for money just like that. It's not going to work."

Olivia said, "Wait and see."

Just then a large dump truck drove up and poured into Olivia's front yard an enormous pile of one-hundred-dollar bills.

"Wow," said Olivia. "Look at all my birthday money." Then she ran outside with a large garbage bag and started filling it with money.

"You're too little to have that much money," said her father. "It belongs to me." And he came out with a bigger garbage bag.

"Oh, no!" said her mother. "I think the mommy should take care of this money." And she came outside with an enormous garbage bag.

The father and mother got into a big fight over the money.

Olivia ran inside and said, "Wait a minute. I didn't mean for this money to cause an enormous fight. I'm going to make another birthday cake." So she made a cake, covered it with candles, and made a wish.

Then she took a deep breath:
Ahhhhhhhhh,

and blew out the candles:
Whhhhhhhhhhhhhw.

The mother and father heard her blowing out the candles and ran inside.

"Olivia," said the father. "Did you wish **three** words?"

"NNNNO."

"Did you wish **two** words?"

"NNNNO."

"Did you wish **one** word?"

"YYYYES."

"One word," said her father. "Just one word. Well, that is probably all right. What was your wish?"

"Well," said Olivia, "I wanted something to make me happy, something to keep me busy, something we all said we wanted, so I wished for—a NEW BABY!"

"Now wait a minute," said her father. "You don't know how these things work. You can't wish for a new baby just like that. It's not going to work."

"Wait and see," said Olivia.

"I don't have to wait," said her mother. "When she wished for snow, she got snow. When she wished for rain, she got rain. When she wished for sunshine, she got sunshine. When she wished for money, she got money. Now she wished for a baby. I think we are going to have a baby!"

"This is crazy," said her father. "Olivia, take back that wish."

"Okay," said Olivia, "I'll take back that wish. I don't really want *a* baby anyway—I WANTED THREE!"

Tenth printing, December 2009

Annick Press Ltd.

We acknowledge the support of the Canada Council for the Arts, the Ontario
Arts Council, and the Government of Canada through the Book Publishing Industry
Development Program (BPIDP) for our publishing activities.

Cataloging in Publication Data

   Munsch, Robert, N., 1945-
    Wait and see

   (Munsch for kids)
   ISBN 1-55037-335-8 (bound) ISBN 1-55037-334-X (pbk.)

   I. Martchenko, Michael. II. Title. III. Series:
   Munsch, Robert N., 1945- . Munsch for kids.

   PS8576.U57W35 1993   jC813'.54   C93-094133-0
   PZ7.M85Wa 1993

The text in this book was typeset in Cheltenham
by Attic Typesetting.

Distributed in Canada by: Published in the U.S.A. by Annick Press (U.S.) Ltd.
Firefly Books Ltd.   Distributed in the U.S.A. by:
66 Leek Crescent   Firefly Books (U.S.) Inc.
Richmond Hill, ON   P.O. Box 1338
L4B 1H1   Ellicott Station
                    Buffalo, NY 14205

Printed and bound in China.

visit us at: **www.annickpress.com**
visit Robert Munsch at: **www.robertmunsch.com**